SNOW WHITE
and the Seven Dwarfs

Illustrated by Mimi Everett

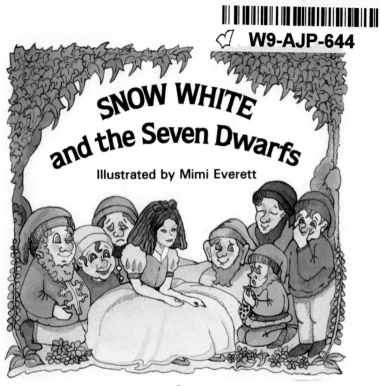

© 1990 Sunbird Publishing Ltd., Loughborough, Leicestershire, England

Printed in U.S.A.

One cold winter day, as the **snowflakes** were falling softly, a queen sat sewing by her window. As she looked out, she thought about spring, and wondered when she would see a **robin** again. Lost in her daydream, the queen pricked her finger, and three drops of blood fell upon her sewing.

The red of the blood and the white of the snow looked beautiful against the black of the window frame. The queen sat back in her **throne** and thought, "I wish I could have a **baby** with skin as white as snow, cheeks as red as blood, and hair as black as ebony."

The queen's wish soon came true. She gave birth to a beautiful daughter and called her Snow White.

But soon after her child was born, the queen died. A year later the **king** remarried.

The new queen was jealous of Snow White's beauty. She told her servants to lock Snow White away in a tall **tower**. Day after day Snow White sat in a **chair**, with only her **doll** for company.

The wicked queen did not think about Snow White again. She was too busy giving orders and making everyone else unhappy.

Every day, the wicked **queen** asked her magic **mirror**:

"*Mirror, mirror, on the wall,*
Who is the fairest of them all?"

And the mirror always replied:

"*You are, fair queen.*"

Then the queen was very pleased.

One day, as usual, the queen asked her mirror:

> *"Mirror, mirror, on the wall,*
> *Who is the fairest of them all?"*

The mirror was silent for a moment, then whispered:

> *"Snow White."*

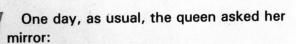

The wicked queen was furious. She said to her huntsman, "Take Snow White into the forest and kill her. As proof that she is dead, bring me her **heart** in this silver **box**."

The poor huntsman was afraid to refuse. He led Snow White deep into the woods. But instead of killing her, he told her to run away.

As soon as Snow White had gone, the huntsman took his **knife** from his **belt**. He killed a **deer** and put its heart in the silver box to take back to the queen.

Alone and frightened, Snow White wandered through the dark forest. Finally she came to a little cottage. No one answered when she knocked on the door, so she tiptoed inside.

Lighting a **lantern**, Snow White looked around. "What a messy cottage!" she exclaimed.

Snow White set to work, cleaning the kitchen first. She washed the seven **bowls**, seven **spoons**, seven **mugs**, and a pan with burnt porridge in it.

"Someone will be hungry after eating burnt porridge for breakfast," Snow White said. So she made some soup and set the table.

After washing the windows and sweeping the **rug**, Snow White made the seven beds and folded the seven nightshirts. By then she was so tired that she curled up and fell asleep. She didn't know that the seven dwarfs were on their way home from their gold mine, deeper in the forest.

When the dwarfs opened the **door** of their **cottage**, they couldn't believe their eyes. Everything was so clean, and a delicious smell was coming from a **pot** on the stove. Imagine their surprise when they found Snow White lying on a **bed**, fast asleep.

The dwarfs woke Snow White. "Who are you?" they asked. "Why are you here?"

"My name is Snow White," she replied. "I'm here because my wicked stepmother wants to kill me."

"Stay with us," said the dwarfs. "We'll keep you safe."

"Oh, thank you!" Snow White exclaimed.

Meanwhile, the huntsman had returned to the palace. Seeing the silver box, the wicked queen rushed to the mirror and cried:

> *"Mirror, mirror, on the wall,*
> *Who is the fairest of them all?"*

And the mirror replied:

> *"In a little house, far over the hill,*
> *Snow White is there, living still."*

The queen ordered the huntsman to be
[thr]own into the deepest dungeon, with only
[sta]le **bread** to eat.

Then the queen, who was really a **witch**,
[ch]anged herself into an old **woman**. She
[pic]ked up a **basket** and made her way to the
[dw]arfs' cottage.

At the cottage, Snow White was baking **cookies**. Suddenly an old woman peered in through the **curtains**. Snow White nearly jumped out of her **shoes** in fright.

"Try one of my sweet, juicy **apples**," croaked the woman. "Just try one, my pretty."

"They do look delicious," said Snow White.

Snow White took a bite of an apple.
Suddenly she fell to the floor as if she were
dead.

The wicked queen laughed. The apples were
poisoned! She turned herself into a crow and
flew home.

When the dwarfs found Snow White, they carried her upstairs, lit **candles** around her bed, and covered her with a **blanket**. They took turns watching her day and night.

Finally, one of the dwarfs said, "I don't think she's ever going to wake up." The other dwarfs nodded sadly.

The dwarfs made a beautiful glass case for Snow White. With tears in their eyes, four dwarfs carried her to a sunny glade. They set her down amidst the **flowers** and left her there for the **rabbits** and other woodland creatures to gaze on.

Many years passed. Then, one bright spring day, a handsome prince came riding through the forest. When he saw Snow White, he stopped. She looked so lovely that he lifted the lid of the glass case and kissed her. At that moment, Snow White opened her eyes. The witch's spell was broken!

The dwarfs told the prince what had happened. After hearing the sad story, he turned to Snow White and said, "Will you marry me?"

"Oh, yes," said Snow White.

Snow White and the prince rode off on the prince's **horse**. The dwarfs followed them all the way to the prince's **castle**, and watched until they were safe inside. Then they took their **picks** and **shovels** and went home.

Everyone, even Snow White's evil stepmother, was invited to the wedding. Wearing her **crown** and her finest **dress** and **cape**, the wicked queen asked her mirror who was the fairest of them all.

"*The bride*," replied the mirror.

The queen stormed out of the palace. Arriving at the wedding, the queen recognized Snow White. She threw down her **gift** and said, "I'll get rid of you yet, my pretty!"

At once, the prince called for a guard. "Take that woman to the deepest dungeon," he ordered.

The queen could not escape from the dungeon, and she soon died there. As for Snow White, her prince, and the seven dwarfs, they all lived happily ever after.

THE END